The Green Fairies

Special thanks to
Narinder Dhami

ORCHARD BOOKS
338 Euston Road, London NW1 3BH
Orchard Books Australia
Level 17/207 Kent Street, Sydney, NSW 2000

A Paperback Original
First published in 2009 by Orchard Books.

A CIP catalogue record for this book is available
from the British Library.

ISBN 978 1 40830 474 7
9 10

Printed in Great Britain

The paper and board used in this paperback are natural recyclable
products made from wood grown in sustainable forests. The
manufacturing processes conform to the environmental regulations
of the country of origin.

Orchard Books is a division of Hachette Children's Books,
an Hachette UK company

Nicole
the Beach
Fairy

by Daisy Meadows

ORCHARD

The fairies must be in a dream
If they think they can be called "green".
My goblin servants are definitely greenest
And I, of course, am by far the meanest.

Seven fairies out to save the Earth?
This idea fills me with mirth!
I'm sure the world has had enough
Of fairy magic and all that stuff.

So I'm going to steal the fairies' wands
And send them into human lands.
The fairies will think all is lost
Defeated again, by me, Jack Frost!

Contents

Time for Action

"Isn't it wonderful to be back on Rainspell Island again, Rachel?" Kirsty Tate said happily, gazing out over the shimmering, blue-green sea. "It hasn't changed a bit!"

Rachel Walker, Kirsty's best friend, nodded. "Rainspell is still as beautiful as ever, isn't it?" she replied, as the two girls followed the rocky path down to the beach. "This is one of the most special places in the whole world!"

The Tates and the Walkers were spending the half-term holiday on Rainspell Island. Although it was autumn, the sky was a clear blue and the sun was shining brightly, so it felt more like summer. Kirsty and Rachel couldn't wait to get to the beach and dip their toes in the sea.

"You're right, Rachel," Kirsty agreed, her eyes twinkling. "After all, this is where we first became friends!"

"And we found lots of other wonderful friends here too, didn't we?" Rachel laughed.

Kirsty and Rachel shared an amazing secret. During their first holiday on Rainspell Island, they'd met the Rainbow Fairies, after Jack Frost's wicked spell had cast them out of Fairyland. Since then the girls had got to know many of the other fairies, and the tiny, magical friends often asked for Rachel and Kirsty's help whenever Jack Frost and his naughty goblin servants were causing problems.

"This is gorgeous!" Kirsty said, as they reached the beach at last.

The flat, golden sand seemed to stretch for miles into the distance. Seagulls soared in the sky above, and Kirsty could smell the fresh, salty sea air. "Shall we explore the rock pools, Rachel?" she suggested.

But Rachel didn't reply. She was looking along the beach, her face clouded with dismay.

"Haven't you noticed the litter, Kirsty?" she asked, pointing ahead of them.

Kirsty stared at the golden sand more closely. To her horror, down near the sea's edge, she could see a couple of plastic bags blowing around in the light breeze.

There were also some drinks cans and empty water bottles floating in the sea.

"Oh, Rachel, this is awful!" Kirsty exclaimed in a shocked voice. "I don't remember *any* litter last time we were here."

Rachel frowned. "We've been learning about the environment and being green at school," she told Kirsty. "And our teacher says that plastic is one of the most dangerous things for sea creatures, because it can kill them if they swallow it or get tangled up in it."

Kirsty shaded her eyes and looked further along the beach. She could see more litter strewn along the sand.

"Rachel, we have to do something about this." Kirsty had a very determined look on her face. "Rainspell Island is beautiful, and we *have* to keep it that way. We'll need help though – and I know just where we can get it!"

Rachel's face lit up.

"Fairyland!" she burst out excitedly.

Kirsty nodded. Quickly, the girls opened the magical lockets they wore around their necks, and they each took out a pinch of fairy dust.

Rachel and Kirsty sprinkled the
dust over themselves, and instantly
they were surrounded by a mist of
rainbow-coloured sparkles which lifted
them off their feet. The two girls spun
through the air, shrinking down to
fairy-size as they did so.

A few seconds later, Kirsty and Rachel tumbled gently onto the emerald-green lawns outside the pink and white Fairyland Palace. To the girls' delight, they saw that the King and Queen of Fairyland and their frog footman, Bertram, were already waiting for them.

"Hello, girls," Queen Titania called with a welcoming smile. "We knew that you were on your way!"

"Sorry to turn up so unexpectedly, Your Majesties," Rachel said. "But this time we need *your* help!" Kirsty added.

"You're always welcome in Fairyland, girls," Queen Titania replied with a sweet smile. "You are our dearest friends!"

"Now, how can we help you?" asked King Oberon.

Rachel took a deep breath. "Well, it's about Rainspell Island," she began.

Quickly, Rachel explained how she and Kirsty had found lots of litter on the beach.

"And it's not just Rainspell Island," Kirsty added. "The whole of the human world needs help with the environment."

The king and queen looked dismayed.

"We've heard of these problems," King Oberon sighed. "But, although we'd like to help, our magic isn't powerful enough to fix them all."

Queen Titania whispered something in the king's ear, and the two of them talked for a moment in low voices. Then the queen turned to Rachel and Kirsty.

"Girls, we have a plan!" she announced. "Today is the Fairyland Wand Ceremony – and you're invited to join us." She turned to Bertram. "Please tell the seven fairies currently in training to meet us immediately by the Seeing Pool."

As Bertram hopped away, Kirsty turned to Rachel.

"The Fairyland Wand Ceremony?" Kirsty whispered, looking very curious. "I wonder what *that* is?"

Meet the Green Fairies!

Rachel and Kirsty followed the king and queen through the beautiful palace gardens, winding their way through the colourful flowerbeds.

"You're going to meet our seven fairies-in-training," King Oberon explained. "They're at the end of their course in fairy magic, but they haven't taken their final exam yet."

As they drew nearer to the Seeing Pool, Kirsty and Rachel saw seven pretty fairies waiting for them.

"Look, this must be Rachel and Kirsty!" one of the fairies cried, and all seven of them twirled up into the air.

"Hello! Hello!" they called excitedly as they spun around the girls.

"Rachel and Kirsty – meet Nicole, Isabella, Edie, Coral, Lily, Milly and Carrie," the queen announced. Then she beckoned to the fairies, who fluttered down beside her. "Listen carefully," the queen went on, looking around at them. "The king and I have decided that, just for a trial period, you seven fairies will be given a very special task."

"Yes. You're going to become the Green Fairies!" King Oberon explained. "And you'll be helping Rachel and Kirsty to clean up the environment in the human world."

All the fairies gasped, clapping their
hands with delight, and Rachel and
Kirsty glanced excitedly at each other.

"If this is successful, then the Green
Fairies will become permanent," Queen
Titania added. "Bertram, the wands,
please."

Bertram hopped
forward, carrying a tray
holding seven glittering
wands. But Rachel
and Kirsty could
see that
the wands
weren't *quite*
as sparkly as
all the others
they'd seen
before.

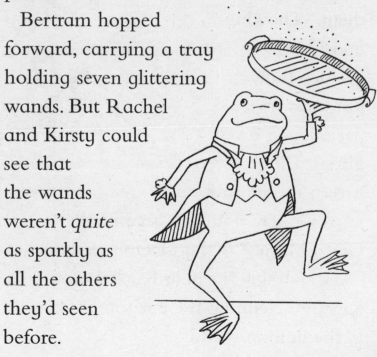

"The wands won't be full of magic until the fairies pass their final exam," the king told the girls when he noticed them staring at the tray.

The queen reached for the first wand. "The Seeing Pool will match each fairy to their special assignment," she said with a smile. Then she touched the wand to the smooth, glassy surface of the Seeing Pool.

Immediately, tiny ripples began to spread across the water. The ripples grew bigger and bigger until a picture appeared.

"It's the beach at Rainspell Island!" Kirsty exclaimed.

The queen turned to the first fairy, who was peering into the Seeing Pool. She had blonde hair tied up in a ponytail, and she wore a red T-shirt, a swishy pink and orange skirt decorated with shells, and flip-flops.

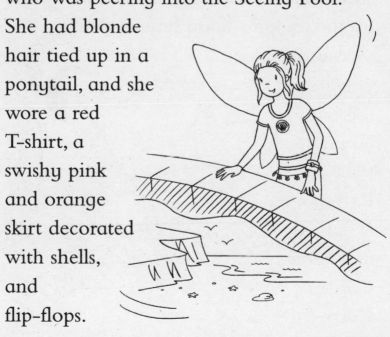

"Nicole, you are the Beach Fairy!" the queen declared, replacing the wand on the tray.

"Yes, Your Majesty," Nicole replied with a big smile.

One by one, the queen touched the remaining wands to the Seeing Pool, calling out each fairy's special task as she did so.

"Air for Isabella, Garden for Edie, Reef for Coral, Rainforest for Lily, River for Milly and Snow Cap for Carrie."

The fairies were looking very excited now.

"The Green Fairies won't be able to *cure* the environmental problems in your human world," Queen Titania explained, "as that is the responsibility of *all* creatures on the Earth, especially humans." She smiled at Rachel and Kirsty. "But they'll help as much as they can."

"That's brilliant!" Rachel said, thrilled, and Kirsty nodded eagerly.

The king stepped forward.

"It's time for the Fairyland Wand Ceremony," he proclaimed. "Each fairy will now be presented with her wand—"

Suddenly, a freezing gust of icy wind swept through the palace gardens, chilling everyone to the bone. Rachel and Kirsty cried out in horror as they saw a tall, thin figure zipping straight towards them, riding along on the frosty blast. He was surrounded by seven cackling green goblins.

"Oh no!" Rachel shouted. "It's Jack Frost!"

The Goblins Go Green!

Jack Frost whizzed down to the ground, a cold sneer on his face. He snapped his icy fingers, and immediately the goblins rushed over to Bertram. The frog footman tried to shield the tray from them, but it was no good. The goblins circled him and grabbed the Green Fairies' wands with hoots of glee.

"Stop that!" the king shouted.

Jack Frost ignored him. He pointed his own wand at the goblins and sent an ice bolt shooting towards them. The next second, the goblins and the wands vanished in a flurry of snowflakes.

Spinning around, Jack Frost aimed another ice bolt at the Seeing Pool. It shot into the water with a splash, freezing the whole pool immediately.

Jack Frost burst out laughing. "That's better!" he yelled triumphantly. "Green

Fairies? There are too many fairies
buzzing around here already!
The world doesn't need any more
do-gooders—"

"We're just
trying to be
green," Kirsty
spoke up bravely.

"Green?" Jack
Frost snorted in
disgust. "Being green
isn't that hard – goblins do
it without even thinking about it!"

"Kirsty means that we're trying to help
the human world become a cleaner and
better place to live," the king said sternly.
"This is nothing to do with you, Jack
Frost. Please give the wands back
immediately."

Looking sly, Jack Frost put his hands on his hips. "Oh, but I want to help the human world as *much* as you do," he sneered. "And I know that each wand will lead my goblins to the Green Fairies' special places." He chuckled. "I'm sure my goblin servants will give a whole new meaning to the words *being green*!"

And before anyone could speak, Jack Frost was gone, whizzing away on another frosty blast.

"Oh no!" Rachel said, looking very upset. "Jack Frost and his goblins are only going to make things worse for the environment!"

"Rachel's right," Queen Titania said anxiously. "We simply *can't* have the goblins running around the human world with fairy wands! Noone must *ever* find out about Fairyland."

"And we want our wands back!" Nicole added, looking annoyed, and the other fairies murmured in agreement.

"We can all work together," Kirsty suggested. "We can look for the wands *and* help the environment at the same time."

The seven fairies nodded eagerly.

"Remember, Green Fairies, that your magic will be limited because you're still in training," the king reminded them. "But your wands will give you a magical boost if you can get them back from the goblins."

"The goblin with *my* wand will have gone to to the beach at Rainspell Island, because that was my assignment," Nicole said. "Let's go there right away!" She linked hands with Rachel and Kirsty.

"Good luck!" the other fairies cried.

The queen lifted her wand and a shower of dazzling fairy dust surrounded Rachel, Kirsty and Nicole for a moment before it swept them away.

Seagull in Distress

As the mist of glittering sparkles cleared, the girls landed on the Rainspell Island beach. They were human-sized again.

"We'd better find the goblin as fast as we can," said Nicole, who was hovering above them. "He must be around the beach *somewhere*."

"Let's start walking," Kirsty suggested. "There's a lot of ground to cover!"

As they set off along the golden stretch of sand, Nicole noticed the bits of litter strewn around the beach, and her eyes opened wide.

"Girls, I see what you mean!" she exclaimed as Kirsty bent to pick up an empty lemonade can.

"Let's collect as much litter as we can," Rachel suggested in a determined voice, scooping up a plastic bottle.

Nicole and the girls walked along the beach, searching for the goblin. But very soon Rachel and Kirsty had too much litter to carry, and there were no rubbish or recycling bins anywhere.

"I don't have much magic without my wand, but I should be able to help," Nicole said. She snapped her fingers and a tiny shower of sparkles burst around the girls. The next moment, two glittery bags appeared at Rachel and Kirsty's feet, one for recycling and one for rubbish.

"Thanks, Nicole," Kirsty said gratefully. She and Rachel put the litter they'd collected into the bags and then continued along

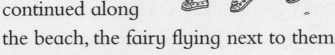

the beach, the fairy flying next to them picking up sweet wrappers.

A little while later, the girls spotted a family sitting on the beach ahead of them. There was a mum, a dad and a little girl and her younger brother, having a picnic. Immediately Nicole ducked out of sight behind Kirsty's hair.

As Rachel and Kirsty passed by, the little girl and her brother jumped to their feet and ran over to them.

"What are you doing?" the little girl asked shyly.

"We're trying to clean up the beach," Rachel explained with a smile.

"Don't you think it would look nicer without bits of litter lying around?" Kirsty added.

The boy and girl nodded.

"We can help!" they cried excitedly.
They ran over to their parents and came
back with their hands full of sandwich
wrappings and empty
drinks cartons.
Rachel opened
the sacks, and
they popped the
litter inside.

"If everyone
did that, the beach would
be cleaned up in the blink of an eye!"
Kirsty laughed.

"We'll *always* clear up after our picnics
from now on," the little girl promised
solemnly.

"Let's go and tell Mum and Dad," the
boy said eagerly, and they dashed off.

Rachel and Kirsty grinned.

"Well, done, girls!" Nicole whispered, flitting out to sit on Kirsty's shoulder. "You're *already* getting people to think about putting their litter away properly!"

The girls walked on, filling their sacks as they went. Suddenly they all jumped as they heard a loud, ear-splitting screech.

"What's that?" Kirsty asked.

"Look!" Rachel gasped, pointing to the water's edge.

A large, white seagull was flapping around on the sand. He had a plastic bag tangled around his feet, and he was tearing at it with his yellow beak, trying to get free.

"Quick, girls!" Nicole said urgently, as the seagull screeched again in panic. "We must help him."

Rachel and Kirsty dashed over to the seagull, Nicole zooming alongside them.

"Hello!" Nicole called, fluttering down to hover near the frightened bird. "I'm Nicole, and these are my friends, Rachel and Kirsty. Don't worry, they'll set you free!"

"That's very kind of you," the seagull panted, as the girls knelt down on the sand beside him. He stopped flapping his wings and sat there quietly while Rachel and Kirsty gently untangled the plastic bag.

"There you go!" Rachel said at last as they finally freed him. The seagull gave a screech of relief and hopped happily around the sand. Meanwhile, Kirsty shoved the plastic bag into her recycling sack.

"Thank you," the seagull said. "My name's Screech, if you haven't already guessed!"

Rachel, Kirsty and Nicole laughed.

"Pleased to meet you, Screech," they chorused.

"Isn't all this rubbish *awful*?" Screech complained, looking around the beach. "I'm not the only sea creature who's getting tangled up in it, you know. Lots of other birds and animals are suffering, too, not just on this beach but on other beaches around the mainland, too."

Nicole's eyes suddenly opened wide.

"So *that's* what my special assignment's really all about!" she exclaimed. "When I get my wand back, I'm going to help clean up *all* beaches."

"Look how much litter we've collected already!" Kirsty said to Screech, showing him her recycling sack.

"Can I help?" Screech asked eagerly.

Before Kirsty could reply, there was a flapping of wings overhead. The girls glanced up and saw another seagull swooping down towards them.

"Hi, Screech!" the gull called. "Do you want to come and play? Bet I can catch more fish than you can!"

"Not today, Beaky," Screech called back. "I'm going to stay with my new friends, Nicole, Kirsty and Rachel, and help them pick up rubbish."

Beaky looked disappointed. "*Everyone* seems to be picking up rubbish today," he remarked.

"What do you mean?" Rachel asked curiously.

"Well, I saw a little green man picking up rubbish and throwing it into the sea," Beaky replied. "He was further down the beach." The seagull pointed with his wing.

"It must be a goblin!" Kirsty gasped.

Goblin With a Wand

"Thank you, Beaky," Nicole cried. "Come on, girls!"

Rachel and Kirsty raced off down the beach, with Screech and Nicole flying along behind them. After a few moments they could see a small figure in the distance.

"There's the goblin," Nicole whispered, "And he's got my wand!"

The goblin was standing by the water's edge, the wand tucked firmly under his arm. He had a pile of rubbish by his feet. As Nicole, Rachel, Kirsty and Screech came closer, he picked up an empty water bottle and tossed it into the sea.

"What are you *doing*?" Kirsty called crossly.

The goblin spun round. He scowled when he saw them, and immediately hid the wand behind his back.

"I'm just trying to be green!" he retorted. And he kicked a drinks can off the sand and into the waves.

"But you're not helping the environment at all!" Rachel pointed out. "Throwing litter into the sea just makes it dirty."

"And anyway, the tide will bring the litter right back in," Kirsty added. "It will end up on this beach again, or on another beach somewhere else."

The goblin looked confused. "You're telling lies!" he said accusingly.

"It's true!" Kirsty insisted.

"Please give the wand back to Nicole," Rachel urged, "and then *she* can use it to help the environment properly."

"Shan't!" the goblin roared furiously. "The wand's mine — Jack Frost said so!"

And he waved it at them menacingly.

Rachel and Kirsty took a step backwards, feeling nervous.

"What kind of magic *can* a goblin do with a fairy's wand?" Kirsty whispered to Nicole.

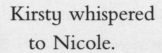

"I don't really know." Nicole frowned.

"These wands are new and have never been used before. The magic in each wand is meant for only *one* fairy – and I have *no* idea what will happen if someone else tries to use it!"

They all stared at the goblin. He was now bunching up sweet wrappers to make a ball. Then he threw the ball up into the air and hit it with the wand, using it like a baseball bat. The ball of litter sailed through the air, landing in the sea with a splash, and the goblin chuckled with glee.

"We have to get the wand back – and fast!" Rachel said. "Maybe Screech can help us?" She glanced at the seagull. "If you feel up to it after what happened with the plastic bag?"

"I'm much better now," Screech replied. "I'd be happy to help."

"Maybe you could fly around the goblin and try to snatch the wand from him?" Kirsty suggested.

Screech nodded. "I'll do my best!"

Nicole and the girls watched hopefully as the seagull soared through the air towards the goblin.

"Go away!" the goblin shrieked furiously as Screech hovered just above him. But the seagull grabbed the tip of the wand in his beak, and began trying to tug it out of the goblin's hand.

"Let go!" the goblin bellowed, managing to yank the wand free. "Get your own wand, you annoying bird! This one's mine!"

Circling overhead, Screech tried to grab the wand again and again. But the goblin was now hanging onto it tightly with both hands. He even began lashing out at the seagull with it.

"Screech is looking tired," Rachel said anxiously, after a few moments. The seagull's wings were moving much more slowly by now. "I think he should stop."

"Come back, Screech," Nicole called.

Screech flew over to them, looking very disappointed.

"I'm so sorry," he said. "You helped *me*, but I couldn't get the wand back for you."

"Thank you, anyway," Kirsty told him. "Now you go home and rest. You look tired."

"I am a bit," Screech confessed. "It isn't every day I get tangled up in a plastic bag and meet a fairy, a goblin *and* two human girls!" And flapping a wing in farewell, he flew off.

The goblin whirled the wand triumphantly around his head.

"Ha, ha, can't catch me!" he taunted Nicole and the girls.

"Now go away – or I'm going to zap you with my wand!" The goblin frowned. "Just as soon as I figure out how to use it properly," he mumbled to himself.

"We're not moving until we get the wand back," Rachel said firmly.

"Well, I'm definitely going to zap you then!" the goblin retorted. And he began waving the wand around, trying to get the magic to work.

Nicole looked very annoyed. "A fairy's wand shouldn't be used to *hurt* anyone," she said. "It should only be used for good magic, and to change people into fairies."

Suddenly Kirsty's eyes widened. Nicole's words had just given her an idea!

A Little Human Magic!

"Rachel, you and I need to shrink to fairy-size again," Kirsty whispered.

"May I shrink you?" Nicole asked shyly. "I've never tried, but I think I have *just* enough magic inside me."

"Sure," the girls agreed.

Nicole waved her tiny hands and a few sparkles of fairy dust floated down around Kirsty and Rachel.

The girls began to shrink until they were the same size as Nicole, with the same shimmering wings on their backs.

"Well done, Nicole!" they cheered.

"Now, do what I do," Kirsty said. She zoomed over to the goblin, and Nicole and Rachel followed.

"Look at us!" Kirsty shouted, hovering above the goblin's head. "You might have the wand, but we can *fly*!"

"Huh! That's no big deal," the goblin said sulkily. "I could be a mean, green, flying machine if I wanted." He shut his eyes tightly and tapped himself on the head with the wand. Nicole, Rachel and Kirsty saw a faint mist of fairy dust swirl out of it.

"Anything happen yet?" the goblin called.

"NO!" Nicole and the girls yelled back, trying not to laugh.

Frowning, the goblin opened his eyes and whirled the wand through the air very fast.

There was a sudden burst of dazzling glitter, and the goblin began to shrink. A moment later, a pretty pair of translucent wings appeared on his green back.

"Yes!" the goblin laughed triumphantly, as he whizzed up into the air. "I can fly just like you!"

"And now we get him so dizzy, that he drops the wand!" Kirsty murmured, winking at Nicole and Rachel.

The goblin was still getting used to his new wings. He darted clumsily through the air, stopping and starting, and almost losing control. Then he tumbled back down towards the beach, but managed to swoop up again before he hit the sand.

"OK, so you can fly," Kirsty called as
the goblin finally began to float around
in slow, lazy circles. "But can you
loop-the-loop?"

And Kirsty whizzed through the air,
completing four loops one after the other.

The goblin scowled. "Of course I can!"
He whizzed through the air like Kirsty,
but only managed to complete
three loops. Then he spun
out of control and
somersaulted head
over heels in
midair.

"What about
this?" Rachel
asked, before
the goblin had
time to recover.

She began doing back flips, then zipping round in circles. The goblin copied her, a determined look on his face.

"Or this?" Nicole said, flying backwards in a zigzag pattern.

The girls and Nicole were now all swooping and zooming through the air, leaving sparkly trails behind them like a fireworks display. The goblin was looking a bit dazed as he tried to keep up with them.

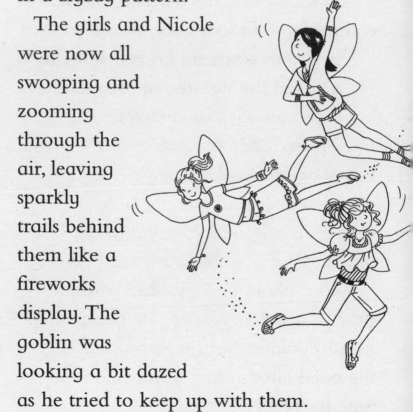

He was zigzagging along in a very wobbly manner now.

"Let's go for it!" Kirsty whispered to Nicole and Rachel.

The three friends began to weave a fast, complicated pattern of big circles in the air, zipping around at speed. The goblin tried to join in, but it was too much for him.

"I'm too dizzy!" he complained. With a groan, he closed his eyes. Then he plummeted down towards the sand and landed with a thud. The wand flew from his hand.

"Thank you!" Nicole said, swooping down to pick the wand up.

Rachel and Kirsty saw the wand begin to twinkle, then it sparkled and glowed with fairy magic. As the goblin opened his eyes, Nicole pointed the wand at him. A burst of magic dust made the goblin shoot up to his usual size, and his fairy wings disappeared. He looked very annoyed.

"Now off you go, back to Fairyland," Nicole told him.

Angrily, the goblin jumped to his feet.

"Horrible fairies!" he muttered,
brushing the sand off.
"Well, you might
have the wand,
but you'll *never*
be as green
as I am!"

And he
stomped
away. Kirsty,
Rachel and
Nicole laughed.

"Thank you,
girls," said Nicole as
another shower of sparkles from
her wand made Rachel and Kirsty
human-size again. "Now I can get
on with my job of helping to clean
up beaches everywhere."

Nicole waved her wand in the air again, and four more sparkly recycling bags appeared. "Here you are, girls," she said, glancing down the long beach. "You've certainly got plenty more work to do here!"

Rachel and Kirsty both sighed as they stared at all the litter lying around.

"Yes, but there's only two of us," Rachel pointed out.

Nicole smiled. "You know what, girls?" she said with a wink. "You have your very own magic to help you! Now I'm off to Fairyland to give everyone the good news."

And she vanished in a cloud of fairy magic.

Rachel and Kirsty looked puzzled.

"Our own magic?" Kirsty repeated, opening one of the new sacks. "What did Nicole mean, Rachel?"

Rachel was smiling. "I think I know!" she replied, pointing up the beach.

Kirsty saw four people coming towards them. It was their parents.

"Mum, Dad!" Rachel called, waving at Mr and Mrs Walker. "Will you help Kirsty and me to collect litter?"

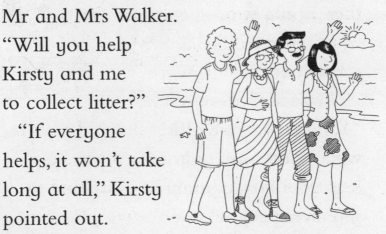

"If everyone helps, it won't take long at all," Kirsty pointed out.

"We'll *all* help," said Mrs Tate as they joined the girls. "We've just been talking about how awful it looks."

"And how dangerous it is for all the sea creatures," Mr Tate added. "Give me a bag, Rachel."

"Let's come to the beach every morning and pick up rubbish, Rachel," Kirsty suggested as all six of them set off with their recycling bags.

"Great idea," Rachel agreed.

"It would be even quicker to clean up the beach if we got more people involved," Mrs Tate said thoughtfully. "Why don't I draw up some leaflets, and ask for help from holidaymakers and local people?"

"I'll give the leaflets out," Mr Walker offered. "And maybe we can organise a group of volunteers to clear up the beach all year round."

Rachel and Kirsty beamed at each other.

"Maybe we *can* make a difference," Kirsty said happily.

"All it takes is a little *human* magic!" Rachel replied with a laugh.

**Now it's time for Rachel and Kirsty
to help...**

Isabella the Air Fairy

Read on for a sneak peek...

"Rachel! Kirsty! Hurry up, we need to
go!" came a voice from downstairs.

"Coming, Mum!" Kirsty Tate shouted
back, putting her hair in a ponytail.
"There," she said. "Are you ready, Rachel?"

Rachel Walker, Kirsty's best friend,
frowned as she gazed around the bedroom
the two girls were sharing. "Nearly," she
said. "I don't know where my shoes are.
Have you seen them?"

Kirsty shook her head. "Maybe they're
in the hall?" she suggested.

The girls hurried down to find their

parents waiting by the front door. The two families were staying in a cottage together for a week on Rainspell Island...a very magical place, as Kirsty and Rachel had discovered the first time they'd been there for a holiday. That had certainly been a summer to remember: not only had they met each other, but they'd also met some other very special friends – fairy friends!

So far, this holiday was proving to be just as exciting. They'd only arrived yesterday but Rachel and Kirsty had soon found themselves in another wonderful fairy adventure, this time helping the Green Fairies in a mission to clean up the world's environmental problems.

Today, the two families were going to Seabury, a town on the mainland. The girls wanted to see a film at the cinema and the grown-ups were going shopping. Kirsty and Rachel really hoped they'd meet another fairy at some point!

Mr Walker looked at his watch. "Girls, we have to leave now if you're going to catch the start of the film. The ferry to the mainland goes in ten minutes, and there's not another one for an hour after that."

"I can't find my shoes, Dad," Rachel said, hunting all over the cloakroom. "Oh, where could they be?"

Kirsty helped her look and the girls searched the entire cottage before finally finding the shoes under Rachel's bed.

"At last," said Mr Tate when they reappeared. "We'll have to drive to the ferry port now, rather than walk. We're already cutting it fine..."

Read Isabella the Air Fairy to find out what adventures are in store for Kirsty and Rachel!

Meet the Green Fairies

Nicole
the Beach
Fairy

Isabella
the Air
Fairy

Edie
the Garden
Fairy

Coral
the Reef
Fairy

Lily
the Rainforest
Fairy

Milly
the River
Fairy

Carrie
the Snow Cap
Fairy

Rachel and Kirsty must rescue the Green Fairies'
magic wands from Jack Frost, before
the environment is damaged!

www.rainbowmagicbooks.co.uk

Meet the fairies, play games
and get sneak peeks at
the latest books!

www.rainbowmagicbooks.co.uk

There's fairy fun for everyone on
our wonderful website.
You'll find great activities, competitions, stories and
fairy profiles, and also a special newsletter.

Get 30% off all Rainbow Magic books at

www.rainbowmagicbooks.co.uk

Enter the code RAINBOW at the checkout.
Offer ends 31 December 2013.

Offer valid in United Kingdom and Republic of Ireland only.

Win Rainbow Magic Goodies!

There are lots of Rainbow Magic fairies, and we want to know which one is your favourite! Send us a picture of her and tell us in thirty words why she is your favourite and why you like Rainbow Magic books. Each month we will put the entries into a draw and select one winner to receive a Rainbow Magic Sparkly T-shirt and Goody Bag!

Send your entry on a postcard to Rainbow Magic Competition, Orchard Books, 338 Euston Road, London NW1 3BH.
Australian readers should email: childrens.books@hachette.com.au
New Zealand readers should write to Rainbow Magic Competition, 4 Whetu Place, Mairangi Bay, Auckland NZ.
Don't forget to include your name and address.
Only one entry per child.

Good luck!

Meet the
Ocean Fairies

Naughty goblins have smashed the magical conch
shell! Kirsty and Rachel must restore it
so that the oceans can have harmony again.

www.rainbowmagicbooks.co.uk